The Emperor's New Clothes

Publisher Cataloging-in-Publication Data
San José, Christine.
The emperor's new clothes / by Hans Christian Andersen ; retold by Christine San José ; illustrated by Anastassija Archipowa.—1st American ed.
[28]p. : col.ill. ; cm.
Summary : A retelling of the Hans Christian Andersen tale.
ISBN 1-56397-699-4
1. Fairy tales—Juvenile literature. [1. Fairy tales.] 1. Andersen, H.C. (Hans Christian), 1805-1875. II. Archipowa, Anastassija, ill. III. Title.
[E]—dc21 1998 AC CIP

Library of Congress Catalog Card Number available upon request from the Publisher.

The text of this book is set in 14-point New Baskerville.
The illustrations are done in watercolors.

10 9 8 7 6 5 4 3 2 1

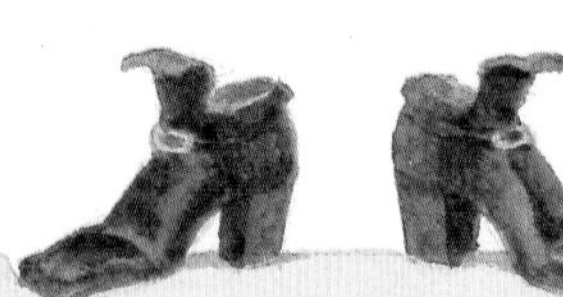

Published by Caroline House
Boyds Mills Press, Inc.
A Highlights Company
815 Church Street
Honesdale, Pennsylvania 18431
Printed in Belgium

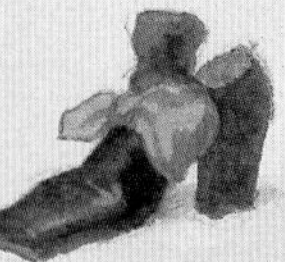
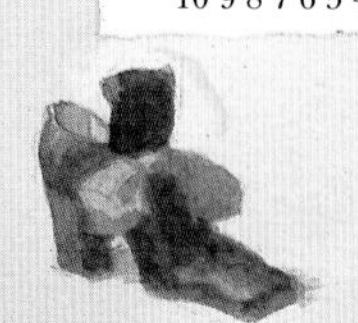

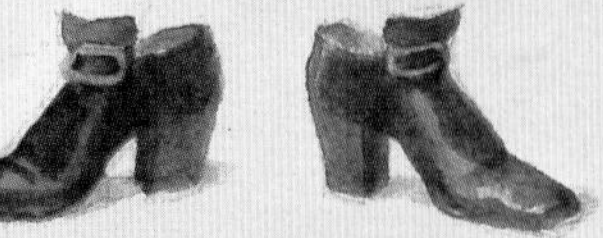

Hans Christian Andersen

The Emperor's New Clothes

Retold by Christine San José
Illustrated by Anastassija Archipowa

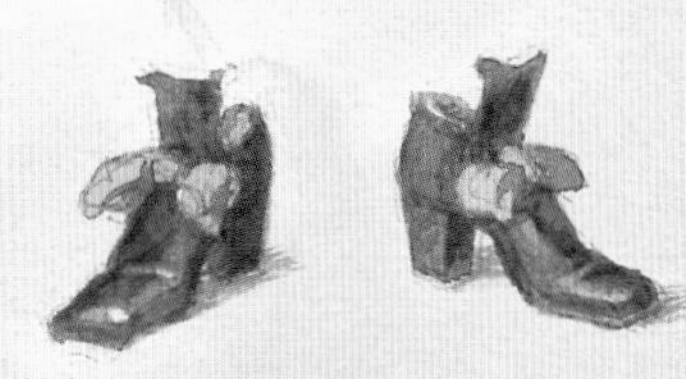

Boyds Mills Press

Can you imagine an emperor—with a whole country to take care of—spending all his time and money on clothes? Well, once there was an Emperor who did. He cared nothing for his soldiers, nothing for music or the theater; he never even stepped foot outside his palace except to show off his new clothes.

Every hour of the day he adorned himself in a different outfit. Any other ruler you would find in his council chamber. This Emperor you would find in his dressing room.

Now the Emperor lived in a city bustling with traders and adventurers from all around the world. And one day there arrived two swindlers. Oh they were weavers, they told everybody, weavers who wove the most wonderful cloth, glorious cloth with undreamt-of colors and designs, magical cloth (and here they lowered their voices) that to anyone stupid was (and here they whispered) *invisible.*

Of course the moment the Emperor heard about the cloth he must have a suit of it. "I shall look magnificent," he informed himself. "And besides," he realized, congratulating himself on his wisdom, "I shall be able to pick out the fools among my people."

So the Emperor gave the swindlers a big bag of gold, commanding them to start weaving immediately.

The swindlers had a sturdy loom set up for them, and late into the night they would thrust the spindle back and forth, as weavers do. But on that loom and on that spindle there was not one single thread.

The Emperor meanwhile could hardly wait to see how the cloth was coming along. But somehow he felt it might be better if he didn't go himself to find out. Of course the cloth wouldn't be invisible to *him,* how could it be?

"But I'll send my wise old Prime Minister," the Emperor decided. "He's a good judge of cloth."

The faithful old Prime Minister stepped into the room where the two swindlers had their shuttles flying. He opened his eyes as wide as they would go, then snapped them shut, then stretched them open again. "Oh my Heavens! I can't see even a shadow of cloth!" he cried to himself in dismay. But not a word escaped him. The swindlers begged him to come close, to capture the full beauty of the patterns and hues.

But the closer the old man came to the loom, the more he could see—nothing.

"Oh my Heavens! Am I really stupid?" he asked himself. "Well at least I'll not be so stupid as to let anyone know I am."

So when the swindlers asked him what he thought of the cloth, he burbled, "Oh it's—it's exquisite. I shall tell the Emperor it's—it's exquisite."

"You make us very happy," the swindlers assured him. Then they pointed out a dozen delicate devices and shimmering shades the length and breadth of the cloth. The minister paid great attention, and later delighted the Emperor as he reported every delicious detail.

Day after day the swindlers would send to the Emperor for more gold to buy their magic thread.

Day after day the Emperor, enchanted, would send it.

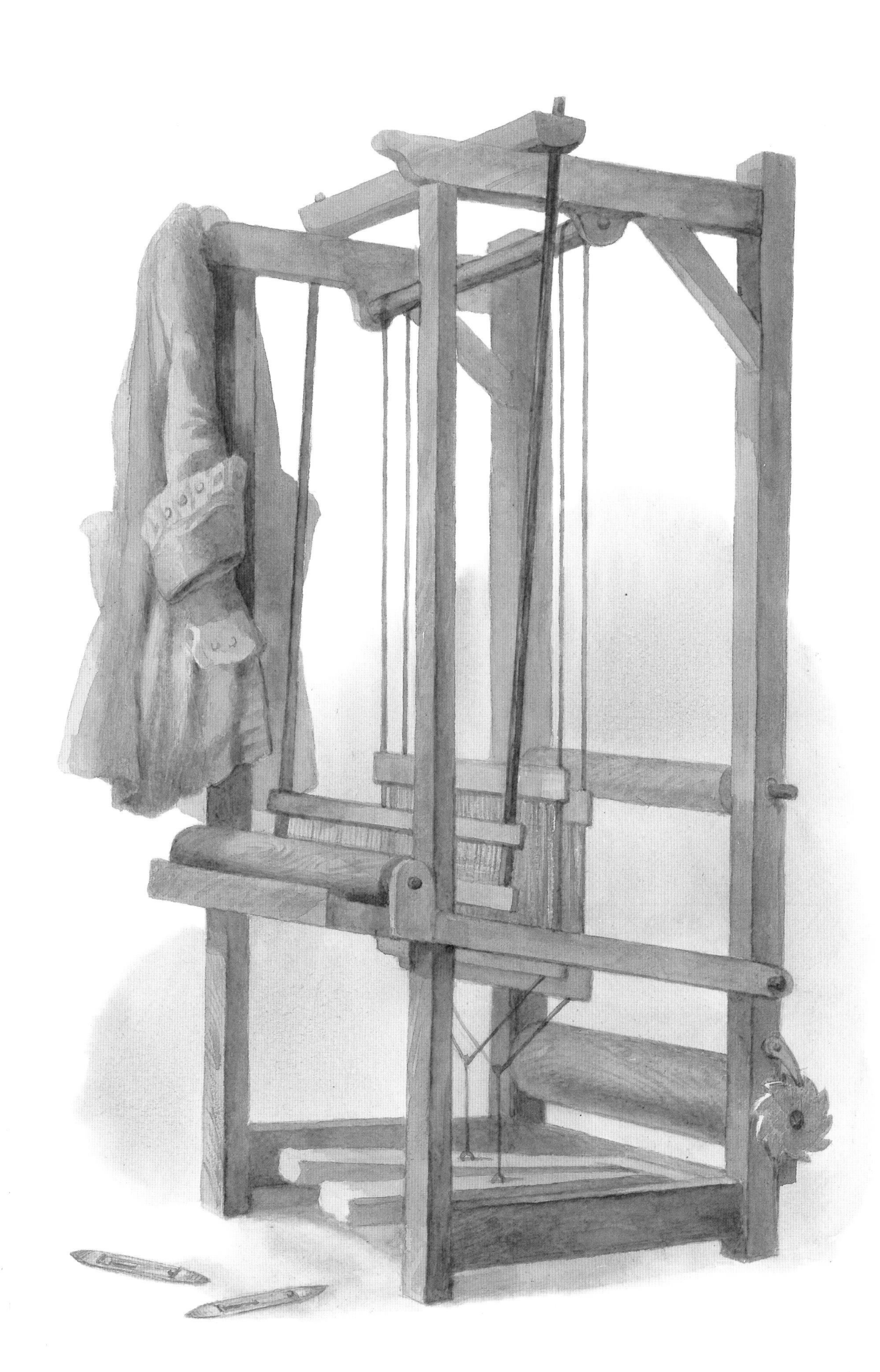

The Emperor now dispatched his Master of the Imperial Wardrobe to inspect the cloth.

This was a quick-witted gentleman. (How else could he have suited the Emperor?) So like the Prime Minister before him he was shocked to see in the swindlers' workshop nothing but the big, bare loom. And like the Prime Minister, he hid his dismay.

"See the hundred greens in the forest we have woven here," said the swindlers, "the perfumed pinks and purples of the flowers, and the snow-white unicorn."

"Oh the hundred greens in the forest!" the Master of the Imperial Wardrobe reported to the Emperor. "Oh the perfumed pinks and purples of the flowers! And oh the snowiest of snow-white unicorns!"

The Emperor seemed to see the cloth with his own eyes! So before he could change his mind—or even his clothes—he ventured forth to the swindlers' workshop with his Prime Minister, his Master of the Imperial Wardrobe, and all his lords and ladies.

"This exquisite cloth is worthy even of my Emperor," beamed the kind old Prime Minister, dearly hoping that was true.

"See the unicorn . . ." offered the Master of the Imperial Wardrobe, careful not to point, sure that it shone snow-white to many people there.

"But I can see nothing!" the Emperor shouted in his head. "This is a nightmare! Am I a fool?" Aloud he managed to say, "It is bare—barely possible to believe any cloth could be so—exquisite."

The lords of the court, who saw nothing but brown boards, trumpeted to each other, "Those greens of the forest!"

The ladies, who saw nothing but imaginary flowers on the empty loom, trilled, "Oh those perfumed purples and pinks!"

Everyone urged the Emperor to have the weavers fashion his robes for the grand upcoming national celebrations.

The Emperor graciously agreed, and he granted the swindlers a special title, "Master Crafters of the Emperor's Empire."

Oh those crafty master crafters! Everyone in the city by now peeked in on them. They saw the crafters take the finished cloth from the loom—at least the citizens firmly told each other they saw the cloth. They saw the crafters measure and cut and stitch the cloth—and firmly told each other the cloth was gorgeous.

And as the celebration day dawned, the robes were ready. The Emperor came with his most distinguished ministers.

“Here are your trousers, Your Imperial Highness,” said one of the swindlers, “and your coat.” “Here is your cloak,” said the other, “with its handsome train.” “Light as spiderwebs,” said the swindlers. “Your Imperial Highness could almost think you had nothing on.”

"Yes indeed!" agreed all the ministers, though they could see nothing, for there was nothing to see.

"If Your Imperial Highness would graciously take off your clothes," suggested the swindlers, "we shall array you in your new ones."

So the Emperor was undressed, and garment by garment the swindlers pretended to bedeck him in his robes.

“Oh what elegance!” cried the ministers. “Oh how excellent the fit! Such colors, such grace, such style!”

“The canopy for His Imperial Highness’s procession awaits,” announced the Emperor’s Master of Ceremonies.

“Very well, I am ready,” said the Emperor. “Am I not excessively fine?” And slowly he turned full circle, looking so hard in the mirror as if he would look right through it.

The two lords who were to carry his train fumbled for where it might be. Then marveling with each other at the rich lightness of it all, they each took firm hold of nothing and processed behind their Emperor out the door.

The Emperor processed under his splendiferous canopy, and all the folk along the street and at their windows called out:

"Just look at that! Did you
ever see the like of
the Emperor's
dazzling new clothes?"

Not one soul there would admit to not seeing the cloth. So they cried, “The Emperor’s new clothes are stupendous!”

But then a little child said, “He’s got nothing on!”

And one person whispered to another, “A child said he’s got nothing on.” “He’s got nothing on!” ran among the crowd, and grew to a roar. “HE’S GOT NOTHING ON!”

Oh the Emperor heard, and was sick at heart. He knew it was true.

“But the procession must go on,” His Imperial Majesty told himself, and squared his poor, bare, shivering shoulders. And the ministers and lords and ladies who followed him kept their eyes on the cloth that was not there.